Produced by The Creative Spark
San Clemente, California

Illustrated by Yakovetic Productions

Printed in the United States of America.

ISBN 1-56326-154-5

# Her Majesty, Ariel

A cool ocean breeze blew across the lagoon, making the leaves on the palm trees dance and sway. The Little Mermaid stretched out on a rock and opened her script. Every year, Ariel and her sisters put on a big show called the Mermaid Musical Extravaganza for their father's birthday. This year, Ariel was going to play the queen.

"Isn't it thrilling?" she asked her friend Sebastian. "It's the lead part in the show!"

"Ah, yes," the tiny crab replied. "I remember once when I was in a play—"

"Could we talk about that later?" Ariel said, interrupting him. "I have to study my lines now."

Later, when Ariel returned to her grotto, she saw Flounder the fish and Sandy, his sister, playing hide-and-seek nearby. "You'll have to find somewhere else to play," she said sternly.

"Why?" Flounder asked. "We always play here."

"Because you're making it hard to concentrate," Ariel complained. "I'm sorry, but you'll have to leave. I have to rehearse for my father's birthday celebration. I'm playing the Queen of the Sea this year, and it's a very important part."

"Queen of the Sea, my fin," fumed Flounder. "More like Queen of the Seaweed."

"Who does she think she is, ordering us around like that?" added Sandy.

That night Ariel kept telling her friends to be quiet. "How am I going to memorize my part when you're all so noisy?" she snapped at them before swimming away to her grotto.

"First she ate all the pickles at dinner," Scuttle complained, "and now we have to be quiet, too?"

"She's acting like she's the *real* Queen of the Sea, instead of just playing one," added Scales the dragon.

"Hmm," said Sebastian, "maybe what we need to do is show her what a queen's life is *really* like."

The next morning, Ariel awoke to find Flounder and Sandy by her bed. They had a tray filled with all sorts of wonderful island delights—there were sweet seaberries, bright juicy oranges, ripe yellow bananas, a coconut, and a bouquet of beautiful sea grass blossoms.

"What's going on?" Ariel asked.

"We brought you breakfast, Your Majesty," explained Sandy.

"Look at all this delicious food!" Ariel said, wiping the sleep from her eyes. "Oh, what lovely flowers. They smell wonderful! This must be a dream!"

"It's no dream, Your Majesty," said Sebastian, appearing at the entrance. "We decided to help you rehearse being a queen. Sandy and Flounder and Scales and Scuttle are all your servants, and I will be your royal announcer."

"How wonderful!" Ariel said, putting on the seaweed crown Sebastian had made for her. "This is going to be so much fun! Flounder, Sandy, I want you to make sure I always have lots and lots of flowers," she commanded. "As many as you can find!"

"But Your Majesty—" Flounder started to protest, but Ariel was so excited she didn't let him finish.

"Come along, Sebastian," she said. "You can announce me at the lagoon!"

"Maybe this wasn't such a good idea after all, Sebastian," Flounder said as he watched the Little Mermaid swim away.

"Just be patient," the wise crab whispered. "You'll see."

Sebastian had to hurry to catch up with Ariel. She was swimming so fast that he was completely out of breath when they reached the lagoon. "Her Majesty," he wheezed, announcing the Little Mermaid's arrival, "Ariel, Queen of the Sea."

"Let me see," Ariel began. "Scales, you're good with music, so you can write me a royal song. And Scuttle, you can fan me with your wings so I won't get hot in the afternoon sun."

"Yes, Your Majesty," they both replied, carrying out her commands. But the breeze from Scuttle's flapping wings blew Scales's music all over the place.

"Hey, stop that!" Scales cried. "Look what you're doing to my music!"

"I'm just following Her Majesty's orders!" Scuttle replied.

"Well, so am I!" Scales snapped back. "She ordered me to write a royal song!"

"Well, she ordered me to keep her cool!" shouted Scuttle.

The wind from Scuttle's wings continued to blow music everywhere. "This isn't at all what I had in mind!" Ariel cried. "Oh, Sebastian! What am I going to do?"

"They're only following your orders, Your Majesty," the crafty crab replied.

Meanwhile, Flounder and Sandy were following Ariel's orders, too. They were gathering up all the flowers they could find and putting them inside the Little Mermaid's grotto.

There were flowers everywhere. Orchids were organized in rows on the shelves. The teacups spilled over with tiny tulips. Hyacinths hung from the ceiling while waterlilies floated in lines on the floor. Every vase was filled with violets. There were so many flowers, in fact, that there was no room left for anything else.

"Well," Flounder remarked as he stacked sea grass blossoms in front of the grotto doorway, "she said she wanted lots and lots of flowers, right?"

Ariel eventually got Scales and Scuttle to stop arguing, but the whole thing was quite exhausting. "Being a queen is a lot harder than I thought," Ariel said as she and Sebastian made their way back under the sea.

"Yes," the crab agreed. "There is a lot of responsibility that goes with being a queen."

When they reached the grotto it was overflowing with flowers. "What's happened here?" cried Ariel. "I can't get inside my grotto."

"You said you wanted lots and lots of flowers," Flounder said proudly. "Well, here they are!"

"That does it!" cried Ariel, taking off her seaweed crown. "I'm through being Queen! This isn't what I thought it would be like at all!"

"But Ariel," said Sebastian, "I thought you enjoyed acting like a queen."

"Being a queen isn't as much fun as being myself," said Ariel. "It's all right to act like a queen in a show, but I don't want my friends to do everything I say!"

"So I guess this means you won't be ordering them around anymore, hmm?" the tiny crab asked.

"I'm sorry I haven't been as nice as I should be to my friends," Ariel said. "I guess I let playing a queen go to my head."

After that, Ariel stopped bossing her friends around. Everyone was so happy to have the *real* Ariel back, they made sure to be extra-quiet so she could rehearse her part for the play. And on the night of the show they were all there, sitting in the front row.

"Wow, she's really good!" whispered Sandy.

"She sure is," Flounder agreed. "She's the best Queen of the Sea I've ever seen!"